Mel Bay Presents

Walking Jazz Lines *for* Bass

by Jay Hungerford

Featuring:

The Blues • Rhythm Changes • Plus 20 Popular Jazz Standards

CD CONTENTS

1 2 3 4 5 6 7 8 9 0

Visit us on the Web at www.melbay.com — E-mail us at email@melbay.com

Contents

This book and CD will give you the opportunity to play with one of the finest rhythm sections around today. The recording is in stereo. Bass and drums are on the left channel, piano and drums are on the right channel. You can listen to the bass lines and follow along on the corresponding page in the book. Then I would suggest you go back to the page with chords only and use the examples to practice. You can turn the bass off by listening to only the right channel. All the standards with the exception of standard #6 and #7 are played 2 times. For the first chorus I played the written lines found in Part Three of the book. On the second chorus I improvised a walking line using fills and added notes (pg. 44). I suggest teachers have their students transcribe the second chorus walking lines. It is great ear training. Good luck and remember; "Don't try to hit a homerun every time, just get on bass."

I would like to thank Dave Venn (piano) and Kevin Gianino (drums) not only for the exceptional job they did on this recording, but for their friendship through the years. Engineer – Dan Kury, Betty and Roger Oliver (Studio 88).

Introduction

Trumpet legend Dizzy Gillespie once called the bass "the most important instrument in any band." Whether you agree or not, it is true the bass rarely receives the recognition it deserves. From classical to rock to country to jazz, the bass supports the harmony, chords and melody. Take the bass away and it becomes difficult for the listener to make sense of the chords and harmonic structure.

As a bassist, you have responsibilities. You must create interesting lines under the chord changes, keep the "time flow" or "pulse" steady and keep the form of the song together. Soloists and vocalists, while being featured, often tune in to the bass to remind them where they are in the form of the song. An occasional missed note or fluctuation in tempo happens to all of us. Getting lost in the form of the tune, however, is a no-no. It will happen and you will pick up tricks to help you get back on track - knowing the melody, having eye contact with the other players, and listening for cues.

This book is designed to help you create beginning to advanced walking patterns. I've used these lesson plans for several years and have seen even the most challenged students grow to become very accomplished jazz bassists. Why learn how to create an interesting walking bass line? You will find walking bass lines in rock, blues, r&b, gospel, latin and country. In virtually all styles of music you need to become familiar with this style. Whether you are planning to play music for fun or as a profession, you'll enjoy it more if you learn to walk. Switching from jazz to rock is much easier than the reverse. Why not become proficient at all styles of music. It is more fun to answer the phone with "sure, I can do that" rather than "well, I only know how to play rock music."

Preparation is very important for any instrument. Having a daily practice routine is essential. Some might like to think the time spent rehearsing with their friends or band is enough. Putting in some time beforehand, even if its as little as 20 - 30 minutes, pays off big. If you are playing pop, rock or latin it is so much easier to lock in with the kick drum when you have put in some time playing scales. Rhythm section players do not have the luxury of taking a solo and then standing off to the side while the rest of the band does their thing. You are usually playing from the moment the song starts to the last note. With the right preparation, your job will be much easier. One of the best musical feelings for a bassist is to be in the middle or towards the end of a fast tune and not be tired. Chops (endurance) are essential. Perhaps the worst musical feeling for a bassist is having to worry about two things - being creative and physically being able to get through the song. You will be amazed how your concentration and creativity increases when the physical problem is eliminated. Your "time" will be much stronger.

In the lessons that follow, you need to transpose the patterns. This means play all patterns in all keys. By doing this you will not only be committing the patterns to memory, you will be learning your instrument as well. This is a little trickier for upright players because there are no frets. Don't give up. Do the math (intervals). You will find it gets easier and easier. For those that play only electric bass, memorize a fingering. After you become comfortable, try the exercises in first position (using only the first four frets and open strings). This will come in handy when/if you should decide to switch to upright in the future.

You must listen to jazz. I'm not saying listen only to this style, but include jazz in your music library. Occasionally students will come to a lesson with a blank expression on their face and say they are having trouble applying what we've talked about. After asking what they listen to (or what they don't listen to), you can guess the rest. Get play-along recordings. They are a wonderful tool. You can take the bass track off and play with the recording. It is also a good idea to play along with real recordings. Play everything you learn in all keys. This will show you your weaknesses. We all have weaknesses and often like to ignore them. Let them be your guide in knowing what to practice. Some lessons in this book are more difficult than others and will require a little more effort. Don't become frustrated, spend a little extra time on the more difficult patterns. The results will be worth your effort.

Notes On The Fingerboard

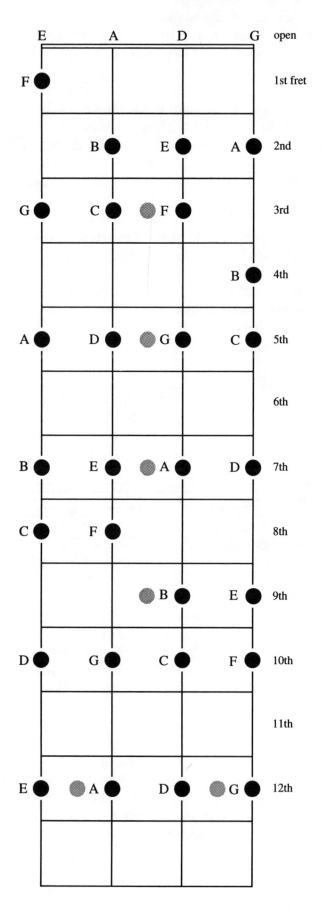

This illustration shows where all the natural notes are found on the fingerboard. Study it and then find the notes on your instrument. If you are just starting out, spend at least 5 minutes a day reviewing the chart.

Remember: The space between the notes E-F and B-C is a half-step (one fret). All the rest are whole steps (two frets).

The Open Strings

Notes On The Lines

Notes On The Spaces

Notes On The Staff

1st String - G

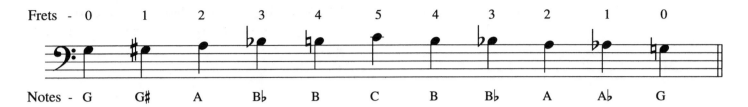

2nd String - D

3rd String - A

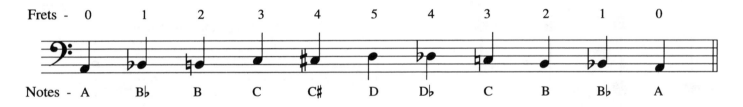

4th String - E

Basic Intervals

The Major Scale

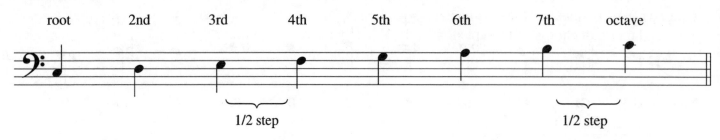

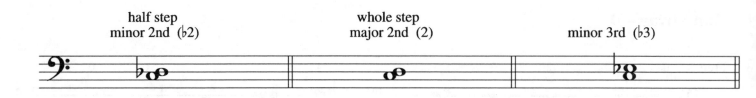

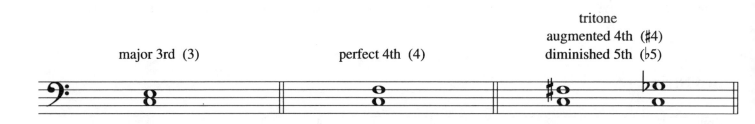

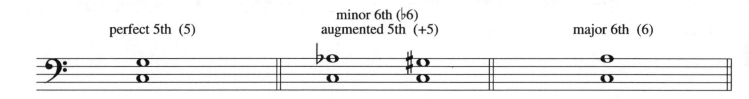

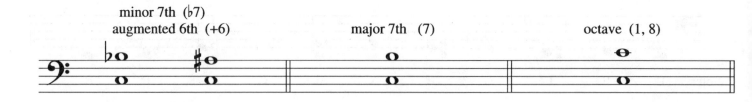

Basic Chord Structure

A chord can be defined as "the simultaneous sounding of three or more tones." It is important to study these triads and four part chords and be able to identify them by their corresponding symbols.

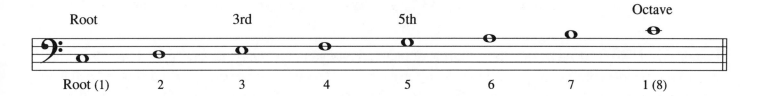

A triad is a three-note chord in which there exists a root, 3rd and 5th.

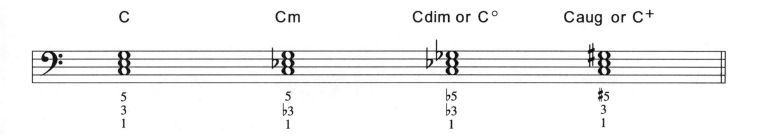

Listen to the sound quality of these three and four part chords. With practice, they will become familiar to you.

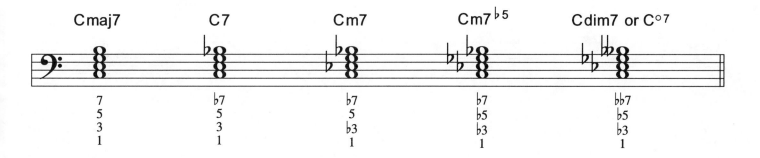

The Major Scale

Practice the C major scale by thinking in terms of intervals. As you play the scale, say "one - two - three" etc. After you become comfortable with the scale, try mixing the intervals to form patterns. You should be able to remember the correct name of the note AND get into the habit of referring to the note by its corresponding number or interval. Now we will start constructing patterns using the notes in the scale. Play each example several times and listen to how they are constructed.

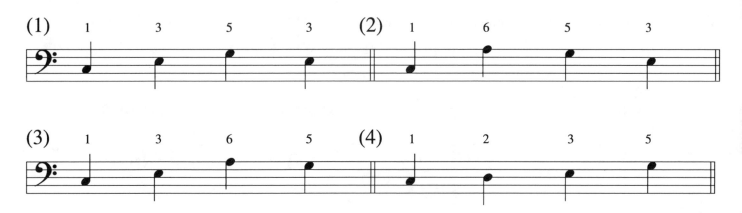

The next 4 examples include notes that have been altered by adding sharps and flats or accidentals. To add variety, you have the option of playing the first note of each example in one of two octaves. NOTE: If you want to make a large jump - make the jump between beats1 and 2 or beats 3 and 4. When developing a walking line, the idea is to take the listener smoothly to the next chord. Beats 1 and 3 are harmonically and rhythmically the stronger beats. After arriving on beats 1 or 3 you can make larger jumps.

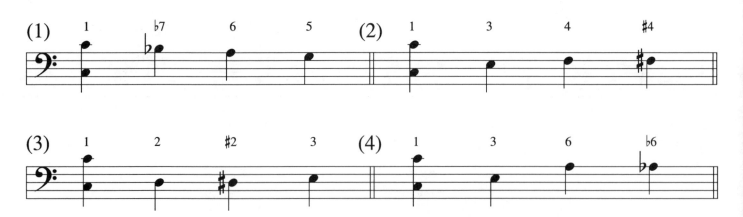

Let's add two more major scales - F and G. Remember, when playing each scale, think the interval or number. It might help saying the interval outloud as you play. Start making it a habit. Thinking in these terms will save you valuable time in rehearsal or in the studio. You will be able to transpose anything you play without rewriting your part.

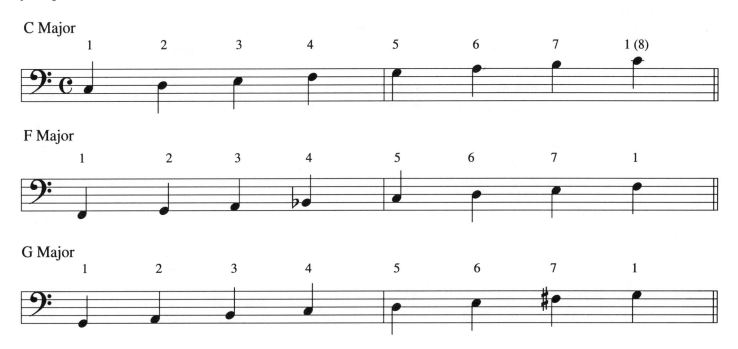

Using the numbers (intervals) practice transposing these patterns using the chord progression at the bottom of the page. For example, 1 - 3 - 5 - 3 in the key of C would be C - E - G - E. If you get confused refer to the scales above for help.

(1) 1 - 3 - 5 - 3   (2) 1 - 6 - 5 - 3   (3) 1 - 3 - 6 - 5   (4) 1 - 2 - 3 - 5

(5) 1 - 2 - 6 - 5   (6) 3 - 5 - 3 - 1   (7) 5 - 4 - 3 - 1   (8) 3 - 6 - 5 - 1

Now lets add a few accidentals (sharps and flats).

(9) 1 - 2 - ♯2 - 3   (10) 1 - 3 - 6 - ♭6   (11) 1 - 3 - 4 - ♯4   (12) 1 - ♭7 - 6 - 5

(13) 1 - ♯1 - 2 - ♭2   (14) 6 - ♭6 - 5 - 1   (15) 2 - ♭2 - 1 - 5   (16) ♭7 - 6 - ♭6 - 5

The Blues

"The Blues" is not a song, but rather a musical form. It is a twelve-bar form without a bridge or second part. Today, the blues is commonly used in jazz, rock, country and gospel music. The changes have evolved through the years (see pgs. 88, 89), however, many "blues" bands today play the original changes used by our ancestors over one hundred years ago. As you progress, you will be adding-to or changing a few of the chords.

In this exercise you will need to transpose each one-measure pattern to F and G. Take one pattern at a time and plug it into each measure of the progression found at the bottom of the page. Example #1 simply outlines the triad, root - third - fifth - third or 1 - 3 - 5 - 3. Memorize each example before transposing them. Use the numbers (intervals).

When descending, as in examples 7 and 8, be sure to flat the seven as shown. Generally, all chords in blues have a flat seven (♭7).

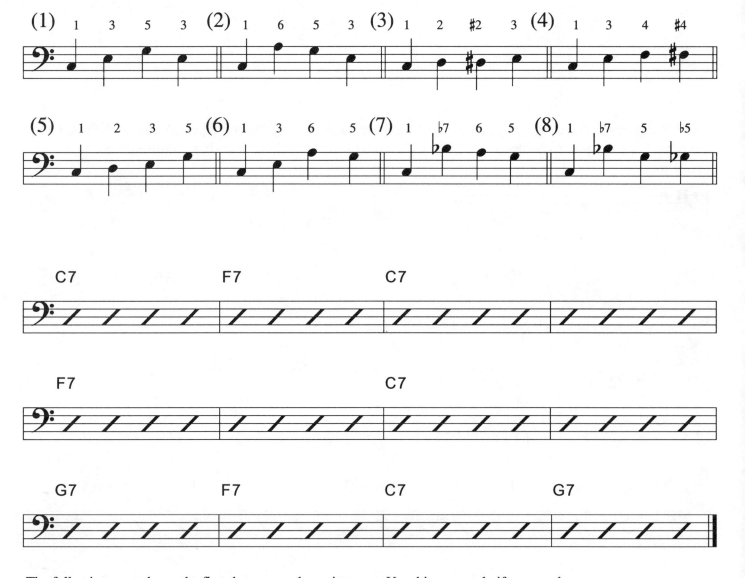

The following page shows the first three examples written out. Use this page only if you need to.

Walking With Intervals

Exercise #1 (1-3-5-3)

Exercise #2 (1-6-5-3)

Exercise #3 (1-2-♯2 or ♭3-3) In this exercise substitute **Dm** for G7 and **G7** for F7 (meas. 9,10)

Adding Two Measure Patterns (Blues)

One Measure Patterns

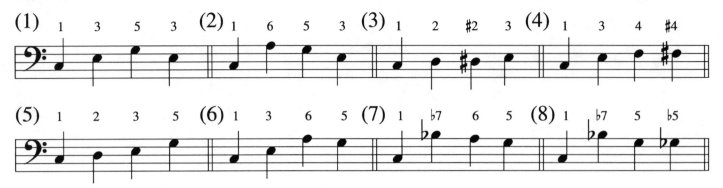

Two Measure Patterns: When only one chord is played over two or more measures, you do not always want to repeat the root (1) on the first beat of every measure. Look for a strong note in the chord (3rd or 5th) to target, then work your way back to the root. You've started your pattern on the root (1), landed on a strong note (the 5th in the examples below) and concluded the statement by ending on the root (1). More examples can be found on page 24.

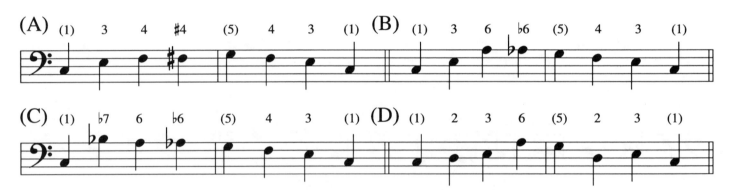

Pick a one measure pattern and place it in measures 1, 2, 9, 10, 11 and 12. You will have to transpose this pattern to the keys F and G. Place a two measure pattern in measures 3 - 4, 5 - 6 and 7 - 8. You will only have to transpose the two measure pattern once to F. When you become comfortable with this exercise, try using the substitution chords - Dm and G7 in measures 9 and 10. When transposing a one measure pattern to Dm (minor), you will need to lower the third one-half step.

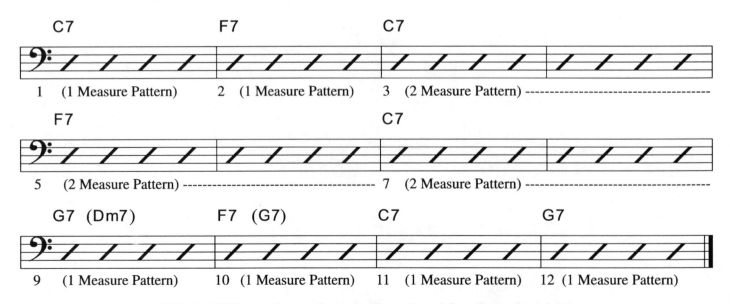

* Make All Large Jumps Between Beats 1 and 2 or Beats 3 and 4 *

Combining One and Two Measure Patterns
(Using Dm, G7 sustitutions)

(1) Combining **One Measure** pattern (#1) with a **Two Measure** pattern (A).

Note: In the next two examples, on beat 4 of measures 2 and 11, raise the 5th to a ♭6th.

(2) **One measure** pattern (#7) - **Two measure** pattern (C)

(3) **One measure** pattern (6) - **Two measure** pattern (B)

I - IV - I Walking Patterns

Don't be fooled by the short form of the Blues. It contains several interesting chord relationships. Look at the first two chords (C7, F7). You want to take the listener from the I chord (C7) smoothly to the IV chord (F7) and back to the I chord. Notice the last note before changing chords. It is usually placed close to the "target note." In the example below, the four chord or F is the target note. More often than not, chords will change on the 1st or 3rd beat of the measure. In making the transition to a new chord, place the last note close to the new chord (usually a whole-step or half-step, above or below). Study the examples below. Transpose them to all keys in the exercise found on the next page.

As you become comfortable with the 1-4-1 progression, look for notes other than the root (1) to start the measure. The next two examples show the third (3) used as a substitute for the root (1) on the four chord (F7). Using substitution starting notes will be discussed in more detail later in the book.

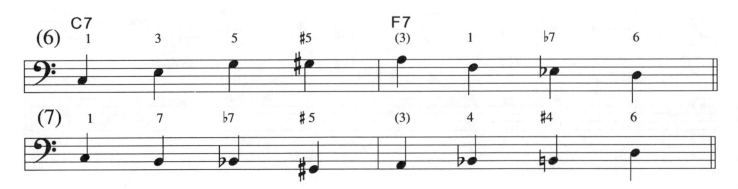

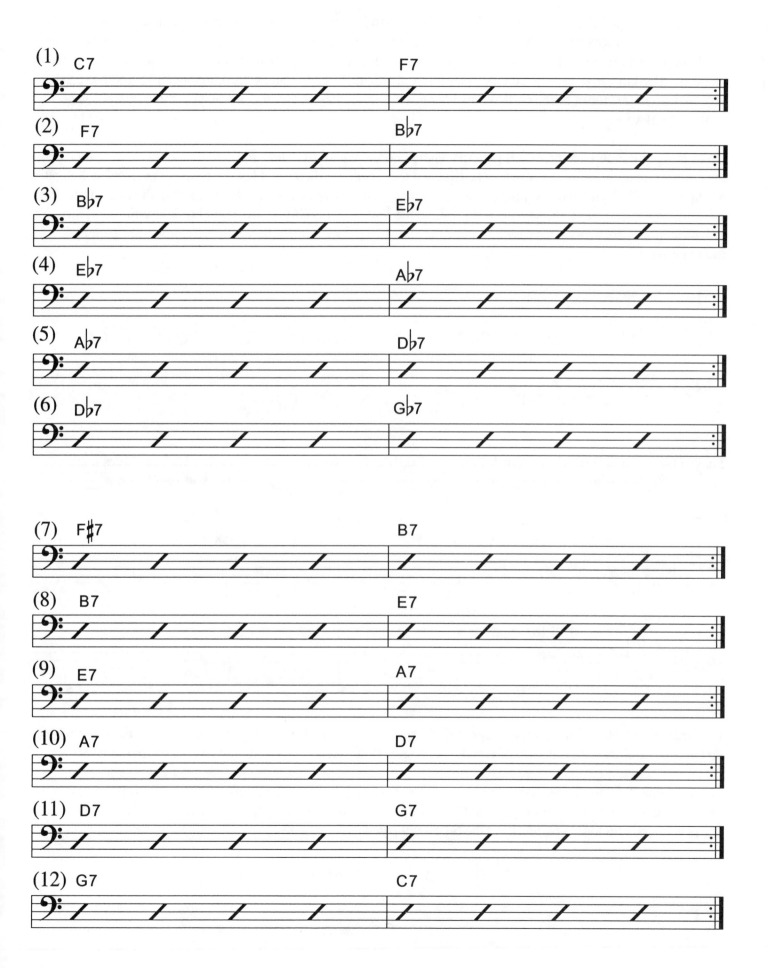

I - IV - I Walking Exercise

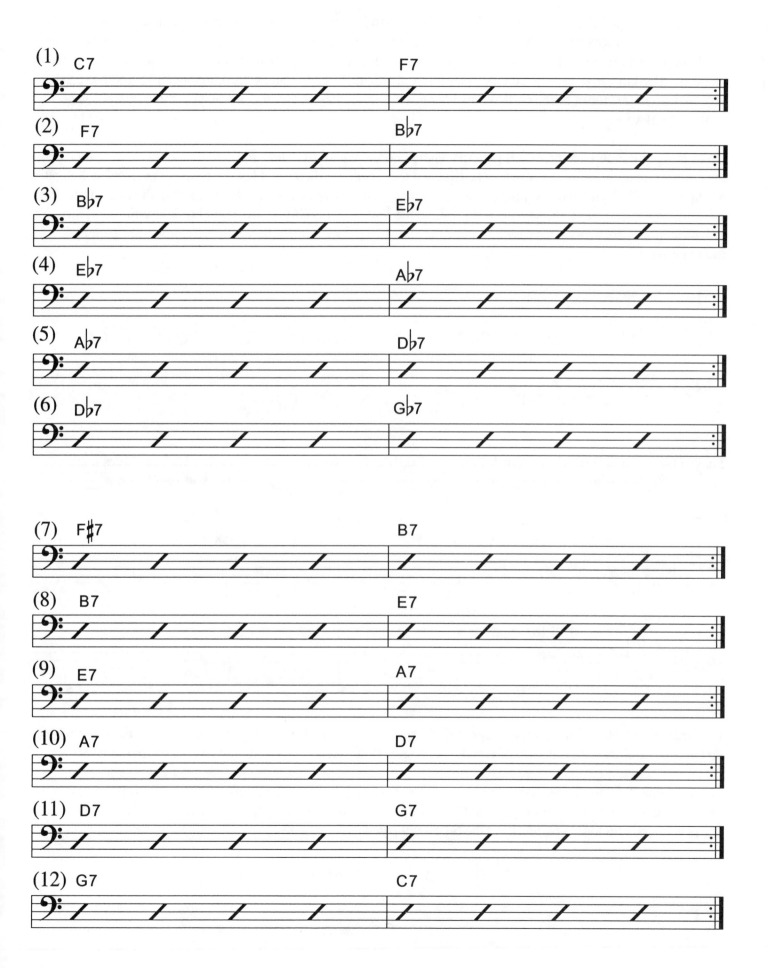

"Rhythm" Changes

One of the most popular chord progressions of the Bebop Era is a form called Rhythm Changes. George Gershwin's "I Got Rhythm" is the source for this popular set of changes. It is perhaps second only to the blues. Many popular composers, including Sonny Rollins, Miles Davis and Charlie Parker wrote "heads" (melodies) based on Rhythm Changes. The changes are fun to play over. Like the blues, the chords can be altered (page 90). In most cases, tunes based on Rhythm Changes are in the key of B♭, and are played at fast tempos. The form is AABA.

Up to this point, you have practiced patterns where chords extend over one and two measures. You will now see the chords changing every other beat. The first and third beat are dictated. Play the root of the chord as indicated by the music. On beats two and four you have to improvise. There is only one beat to set up the next chord. The exercise on the next page shows four ways to take the listener smoothly to the next chord. Use the root, 3rd, 5th or half-step movement as your passing tones. For the "bridge" or B section, use the "two-measure patterns" found on page 12.

Look at the example below. Notice the variation of passing tones as indicated by parenthesis.

The bridge (section B) contains four V7 chords. Take the four two-measure examples from the blues page (pg.12) and plug them in. More examples can be found on page 24, 'Two Measure Walking Patterns.'

The written versions of this exercise (pgs. 18, 19) shows how to practice using 3rds and 5ths as passing tones. To become familiar with the form of Rhythm Changes, first practice repeating the root as the passing tone. When you are comfortable, move on to 3rds and so on. Use the written versions only as a guide. Use these passing tones (PT) on all songs that have chord movement every two beats. Refer to them often. Below is another example with repeated II - Vs. In this example, the minor chords contain a ♭7 and a ♭5. If you chose a 5th as your passing tone, you must flat the 5th as indicated.

Rhythm Changes Exercise

For measures 1-14, use example #1 first. When you feel comfortable move on to 3rds, then 5ths. Practice one at a time.

(measures 15-24, use the two-measure patterns pg.12)

Rhythm Changes

(Using 3rds as Passing Tones)

Rhythm Changes

(Using 5ths as Passing Tones)

The II - V - I Progression

Perhaps the most important chord progression in jazz is the II-V, which may or may not resolve to I. The majority of songs will have II-V progressions scattered throughout. In this lesson you will study the II-V-I in major keys. In the key of C, the second, fifth, and first notes of the C major scale are D, G and C. The II is a minor 7th chord, the V is a dominant 7th chord and the I chord is a major 7th chord.

Below, you will find four walking patterns in the key of C major. Become familiar with one pattern at a time. They are easy to memorize and will help you when transposing the patterns. There are two ways to practice this exercise. The easiest is to follow a fingering pattern (a suggested fingering can be found under each staff in the examples below). If you choose this method, do not use open strings. By using the same fingering pattern for each key, you only need to find the first note of each pattern on your bass. You will, however, be jumping around the neck. This is fine as it allows the beginner to become familiar with the upper positions. The second and more difficult method is to only use the open strings and first four frets. Sorry upright players - unless you have a fretted upright you have to use this method. It's a little tougher, but you will really get to know the patterns.

☞ REMEMBER: ALWAYS MAKE LARGE JUMPS BETWEEN BEATS 1 AND 2 OR BEATS 3 AND 4.

Why? Our job in constructing a walking line is to take the listener smoothly to the next chord. Beats 1 and 3 are not only rhythmically, but harmonically the strongest beats in the measure. Once you have arrived at beat 1, you are now allowed to jump to a different octave. When constructing a rock bass pattern you do not have to follow this rule. Rock lines tend to run in parallel motion. Listen to the great jazz bassists through the years and you will find they follow this unwritten rule.

After you become familiar with #1, plug it into the chord progression on the next page. It will take you through six major keys. The note placed on the last beat of each exercise will lead you smoothly to the next key. Note: a hyphen (-) between fingering indicates a shift of one position or fret.

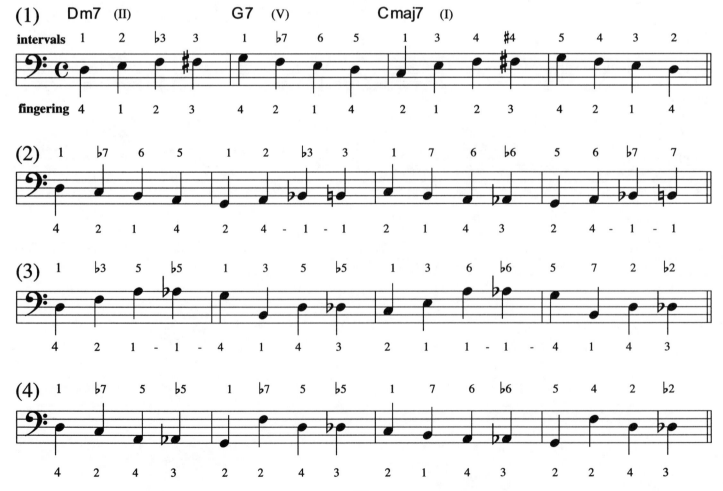

20

II - V - I Exercise

For help, see pages 22 and 23.

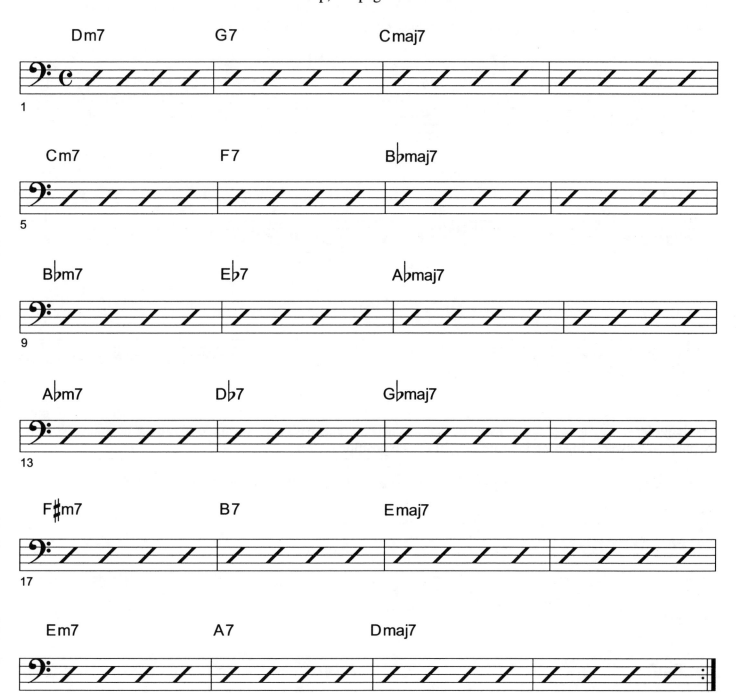

II - V - I Walking Exercise #1

This is a written version of example #1 on page 20. Use it only to check your transpositions. In order to keep the exercise close to the staff, a large jump was made on the second beat of measure 18.

II - V - I Walking Exercise #2

This is a written version of example #2 on page 20.

Two Measure Walking Patterns (C7)

Here are more examples of walking patterns that can be used over chords extending two or more measures. The first four examples can be found earlier in the book. These are designed to be played over a dominant 7th chord but can be easily altered to work with a major 7th chord. In examples 3, 7 and 16, change the ♭7 to a major 7. Copy this page and use it as a reference as you create your lines.

* Pick a note that leads smoothly to the next chord.

Standard #1

(Similar to "A Train")

This familiar standard provides an opportunity to link together patterns found on the previous page. Start by using only one pattern. Play it as written for measures 1 and 2. **When descending from a major 7 chord (Cmaj7), change the flat 7 to a natural 7.** Use the same pattern for measures 3 and 4. You will need to transpose the pattern up one whole step for D7. Use the pattern again for the Fmaj7 making the necessary transposition. You have the option of choosing a note at the end of each pattern. Pick a note that will lead smoothly to the next pattern or chord. One whole-step or half-step above or below the target note will work well. If you descend from Fmaj7, remember to change the flat seven to a natural seven. Refer to the II-V-I exercise for measures 5 and 6. Measures 7 and 8 gives you the opportunity to apply the examples discussed in the Rhythm Changes exercise (pgs. 16-17). If you need help or ideas, refer to page 68.

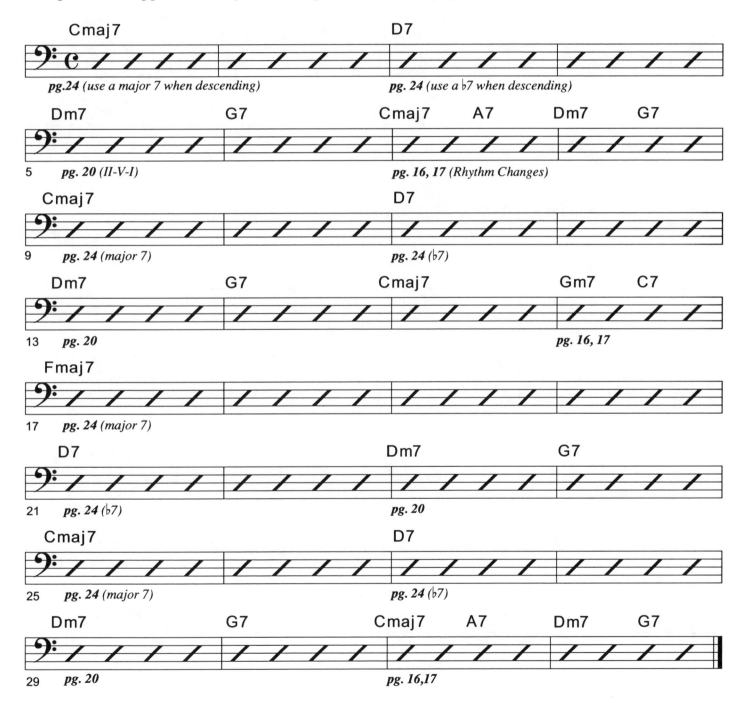

Minor Walking Patterns (Dm)

Modal jazz often contains few chords with lots of space. Miles Davis' "So What" has only two chords, Dm and Ebm. Because there is so much time on each chord, it is easy to "get lost" in the form. Start with only the first four examples on this page. Memorize them. Switch them around. Try substituting the second measure of example (2) with the second measure of example (1). There are unlimited possibilities. When doing this, remember to start your substitution on the second beat of measure two. Why? Because large jumps are more commonly made on the second beat. Practice a few of these patterns without music. When you are comfortable, plug the patterns into the changes on the next page. You will have to transpose each example up one half step for Ebm. Refer to page 69.

Standard #2

(Similar to "So What")

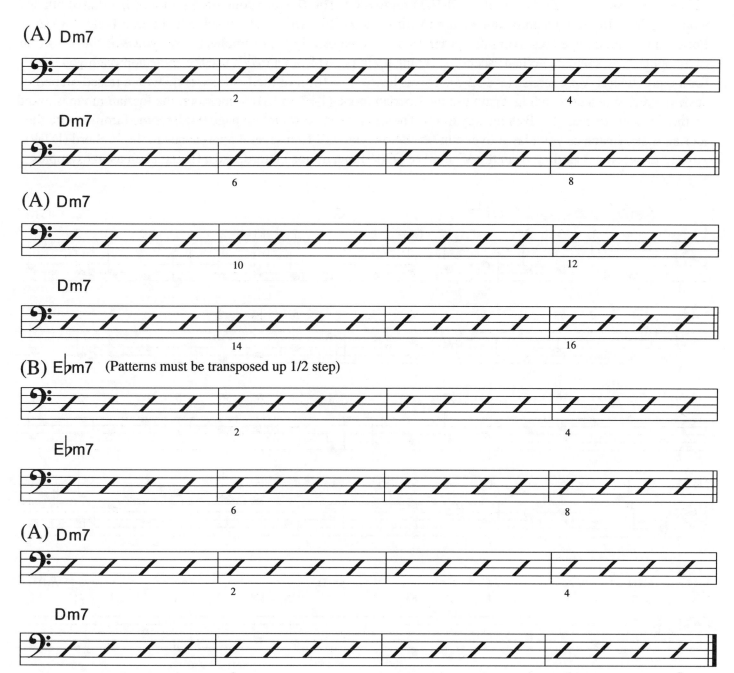

II - V - I (Minor)

This exercise shows another form of the II-V-I progression. The II chord contains a minor 3rd, a flatted 5th and a minor 7th, followed by a dominant V chord with a flat 9. This will usually resolve to a minor I chord. Cole Porter, however, enjoyed resolving this progression to a major I. In the examples below, you will find a section of a popular jazz standard. When ascending (going up in pitch) from a m7♭5, use the same approach you used for the previous II-V-I exercise (1-2-♭3-3). This is based on a form of the Locrian mode with a raised second scale degree. When descending, again use the Locrian mode (1-♭7-♭6-♭5). Remember, the locrian mode is based on the 7th scale degree (B - B in the key of C). The modes can be found on page 94. Become familiar with the locrian scale. Listen as you play it over a m7♭5. Below you will find several approaches to the V chord (D7♭9). Also note, when descending from the V chord or D7(♭9) to a minor I chord, use a flatted sixth as in examples #1, 3 and 6.

28

Standard #3

(Similar to "Autumn Leaves")

This well known standard provides an opportunity to practice the II-V-I (minor) sequence. Use examples 1 through 4 found on the previous page for measures 5-8 and 17-20. For measures 13 - 16, examples 5 through 8 work nicely. For measures 1 and 2, refer to the II-V-I (major) page for ideas (pg. 20). The chord relationship between measure 4 and 5 is new. When walking up or down to a sharp 4 chord (E♭ to Am7♭5), simply walk up or down the E♭ major scale as shown in measure 4 below (pg. 39). Example walking lines for this standard can be found on page 70.

29

3/4 Walking Patterns (G7)

Walking in 3/4 time can be challenging. Most songs are written in 4/4 time. Clapping your hands, marching or dancing is easier when we hear a strong after beat. In 3/4 time the strong notes (harmonically) are placed on the first beat of each measure. Look for notes in the triad to target for your first beat. In examples one and two, the target notes (in this case notes on the first beat) are 1 and 5. In the key of G these notes are G and D. Plug the walking patterns into the blues changes found on the next page. For measures 9-12 you will have to transpose the patterns to the key of C.

Standard #4 (3/4 Blues)

(Similar to "All Blues")

For measures 8 and 12 use the suggested passing tones as indicated by the numbers above each measure. You will also find suggested patterns for measures 17-20. Chords that move in half-steps (D7 to E♭7) will be discussed in greater detail later in the book (pg. 38). For written examples see page 71.

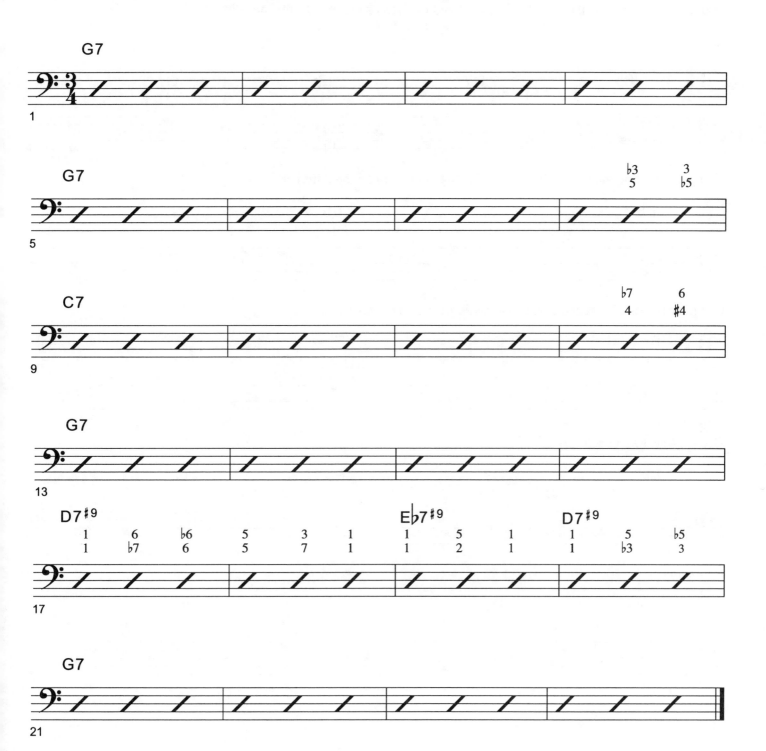

More Examples in 3/4

Often you will be asked to walk in 3/4 time when the chords are changing every measure. The examples below are taken from a popular jazz waltz. In the first example, play the root (1) on the first beat, the fifth (5) on the second beat and the root (1) again on the third beat. In the second example, place the third (3) on the second beat, then pick a note for the third beat that leads nicely to the next chord. In the examples below, the augmented 5th (+5) for D7 and G7, has been eliminated. When walking over the standard found on the next page, you may treat the D+ and G+ chords as D7 and G7. Refer to page 72 for more ideas.

Root - fifth - Root

Using the third on the second beat and a Passing Tone (PT) on the third beat

Using the 5th on the second beat and a Passing Tone on the third beat

Using a linear approach

A mixture

Standard #5 - A Jazz Waltz

(Similar to "Someday My Prince Will Come")

I - VI - II - V

Another commonly used chord progression in jazz is I-VI-II-V. In the 'Rhythm Changes' exercise, the first four chords are I-VI-II-V (B♭, G7, Cm, F7). The VI chord can be played as a minor or major chord. The major VI triad, contains a ♭7 or a dominant 7th, and is used often today but in this exercise you will be using a minor VI chord.

The Rhythm Changes exercise is important because it shows how to find passing tones when chords are changing every two beats. In this exercise you will be using the same I-VI-II-V progression but each chord will extend over a full measure.

You have already spent some time studying the II-V-I progression, so measures 3 and 4 should be familiar to you. The relationship between Fmaj7 and Dm or I-VI, is equally important. It will turn up in numerous songs and may be disguised as a V-III (C7-Am in the key of F) in which case you can use the same patterns. Notice in measure 2 of example #1, the 6th is flat in the descending line. This is because the Dm has the function of a 6th chord. When descending from a 6th chord, use the natural minor mode (aeolian) which has a flatted 6th. When descending from a II chord (Gm in the key of F) use the dorian mode which has a natural 6th. This might sound confusing, but as they say, "you'll hear it."

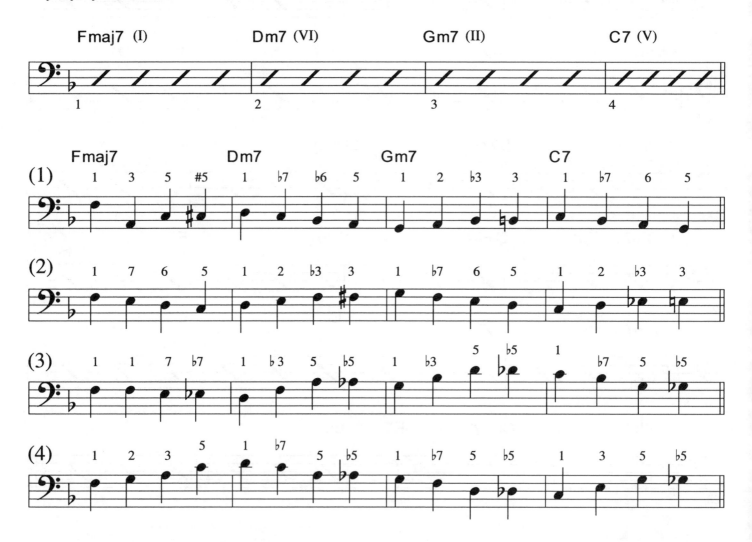

Become familiar with these four examples. Remember, you can exchange measures to come up with even more patterns. For example, take the second measure of example #2 and use it for the second measure of example #1. Use these patterns in Standard #6, found on the next page. For the bridge section, you will have to transpose the patterns to the key of A♭. A new type of chord is introduced in measure 29 (B♭m7/A♭). This is called a "slash chord." The symbol to the left (B♭m7) is to be played over the bass note (A♭) indicated to the right. Refer to page 73.

Standard #6 Using I - VI - II - V

(Similar to "Just The Way You Look Tonight")

Descending Minor

Here you will find four measures taken from a popular Cole Porter composition. Building a walking line under descending half-step motion can be tricky. The first two examples show the root on the first and last beat of each measure. As discussed in previous lessons, this is an easy and effective way to connect chords that are a whole or half step apart. Make sure you are comfortable with this approach before you experiment.

Measure four contains a diminished chord. The diminished scale consists of alternating whole steps and half steps. The diminished chord is comprised of minor 3rds stacked upon one another. There will be times when you must walk or improvise using this scale. Most of the time, however, you will only see a diminished chord in a one measure or two beat situation. Outlining the triad, as in measure 4 of example #1 below, is one way to treat this chord. Examples #2 and #3 show how you can walk using just the first part of the scale, starting on the root and ending on the root.

Use these examples for measures 9-12 on the following page. Remember, exchanging any measure with the same corresponding measure of another example will give you many more options. Spend a little extra time learning these patterns. You'll be glad you did. Refer to page 74.

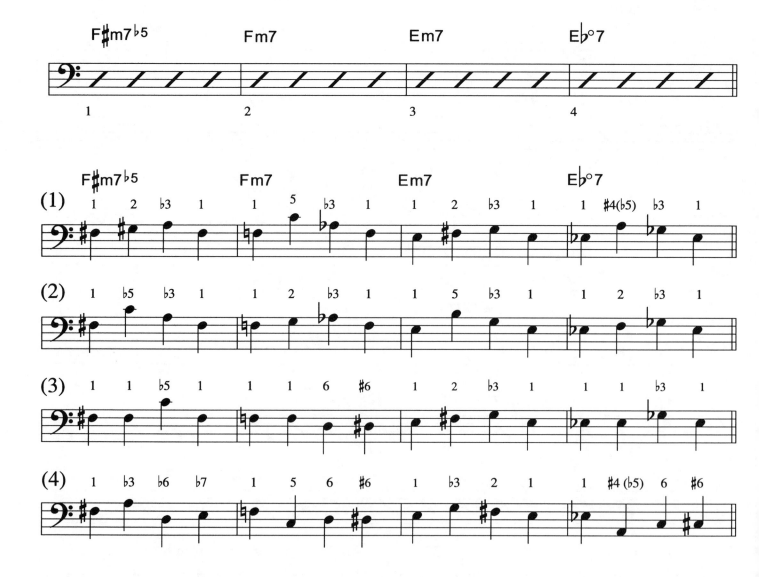

Standard #7

(Similar to "Night and Day")

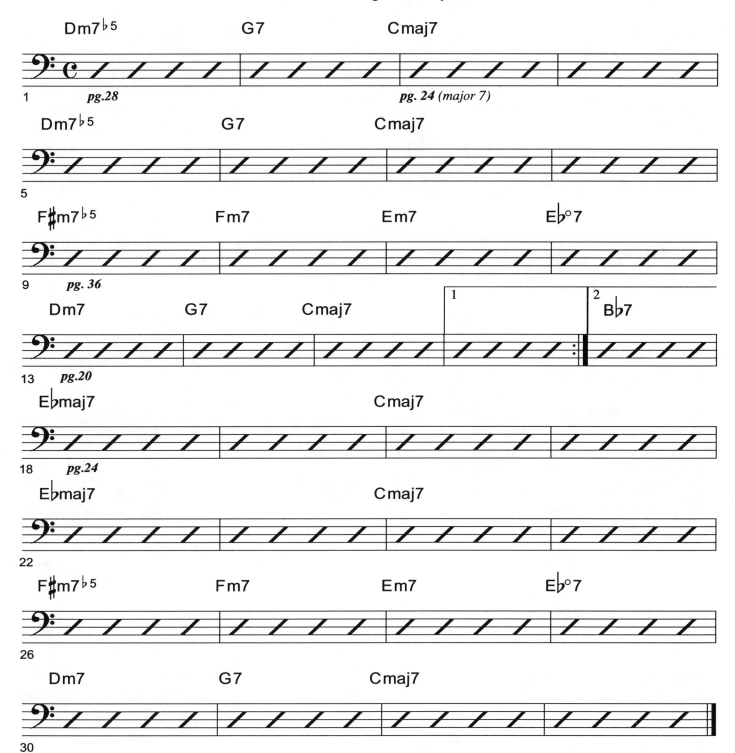

Half-Step Movement

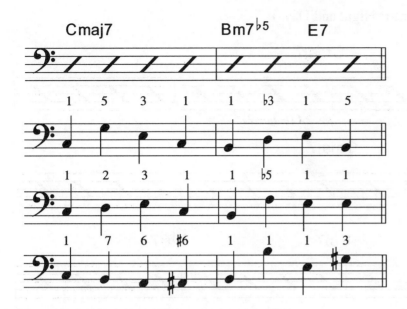

Quite often, songs contain chords that move up or down 1/2 step. Start by placing the root on the first and last beat of measure one, as shown in the first two examples. When you are more comfortable, experiment. For the second measure, use examples from the Rhythm Changes page (pg. 16,17).

This example shows a major chord moving to a minor chord. Use the same idea. Start and end on the root of measure one. The third example shows a different approach. On the Dm target the fifth and walk down to the root. Be creative. Be interesting. Sometimes the listener might lock into the bass. Your job is to not only support the soloist, but keep the listeners' attention. This example can be found in the song "A Night in Tunsia."

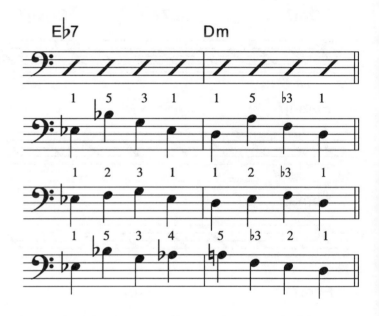

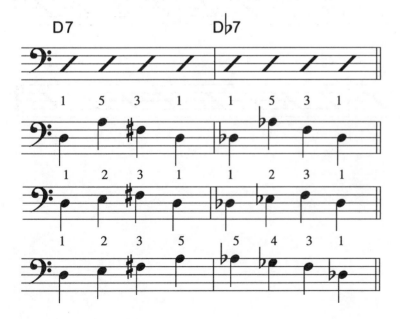

This example can be found in the songs "Satin Doll" and "On Green Dolphin Street."

Uncommon Chord Movement

This example is taken from "Autumn Leaves" in Gm. Am7♭5 is a tritone (sharp four) away from E♭. The solution is simple. Walk up or down the E♭ scale. This will take you right to A, as in the first two examples.

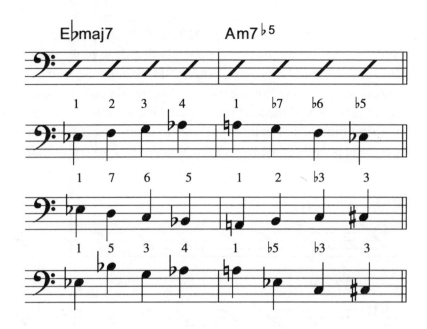

This example shows whole step movement. Again, start off by beginning and ending on the root of the first measure. If you are just learning the concept of walking, applying this idea will make developing a line much easier when chords are moving short distances.

Often students treat this situation as a two-measure pattern. Going from a major to a minor chord implies that a new key center is on the way. It is best to repeat the root of the minor chord. After several choruses, however, you can experiment. Emphasizing the root the first few times through the changes gives the listener the chance to become familiar with the chords. This is a good rule to follow in general. Don't be too clever at first. Save your best stuff.

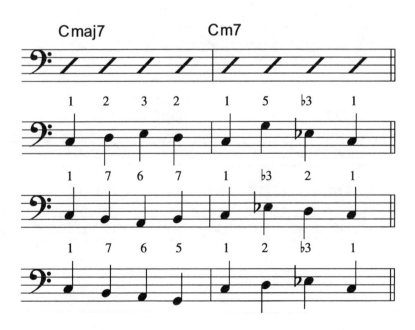

V as a II - V

Many standards written in the 1920s and 1930s contained V - I progressions. Contemporary writers began adding the II chord. At times, you may decide to make your lines more interesting by doing this. Below is the bridge section to "Rhythm Changes." Look at the second example. A II chord has been placed before every V chord. When trying this, be careful. You might only want to add the II chord every other time. Listen to the other members of the rhythm section. Discuss the substitutions with them. If you are playing with a group for the first time, listen to their voicings to determine if you can imply a II chord leading to a V chord. If the piano player is pounding the root of the V chord and you're thinking a II chord would sound nice, use good judgment.

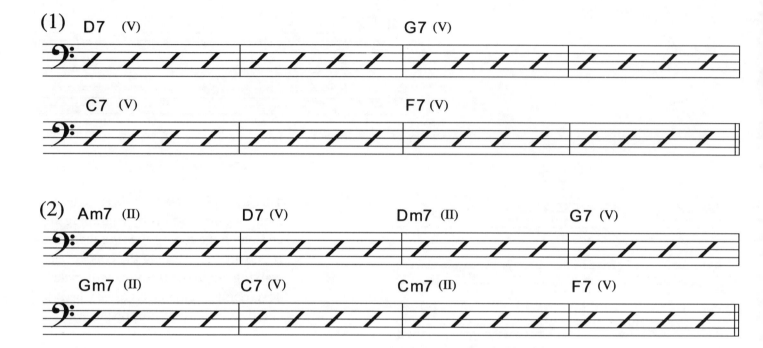

Here are the first 2 bars of "Sunny Side of the Street." Adding the substitute chord (Bm7) gives a more modern sound, creates a II-V and provides more walking and improvisational possibilities.

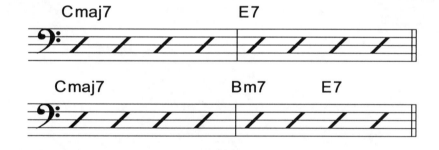

You can turn the example taken from measures 5 and 6 of "Satin Doll" into a II-V sequence.

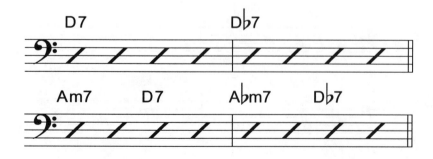

"Blowing Changes" can be slightly different than the original chord changes. As a rule, when "reharmonizing," the idea is to not change the melody. Occasionally chords will be used that do not work well with the melody. These chords are fun to "blow" over and would be used only for soloing. The next three examples are taken from the first five measures of "There Is No Greater Love." The fifth measure (C7) has not changed. The approach, however, has been altered. The second example uses descending half-step movement. The third example approaches the C7 chord by using a series of II - Vs.

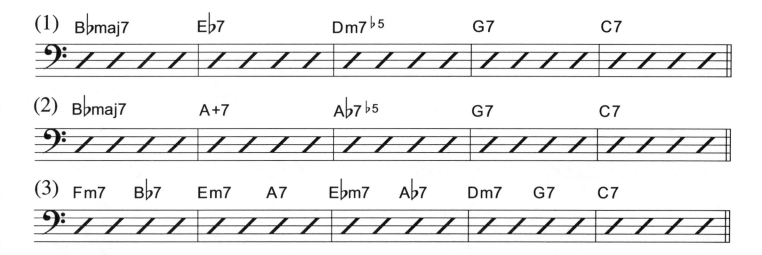

Most of the time jazz musicians are not reading music. We are expected to memorize a standard list of songs (pg. 95). As shown in the examples above and below, chords are subject to change. They might change in the middle of a chorus. Bass players must use their ears and be aware of what is going on at all times. Half-step movement, as shown below, is a common substitution. More often than not, it will happen over a II - V - I. A quick II - V (Ebm7-Ab7) has been added one half step up, followed by a II - V - I in the original key (Dm7-G7-Cmaj7). Becoming familiar with a few commonly used substitutions will eliminate confusion. You will learn to second guess many rhythm players.

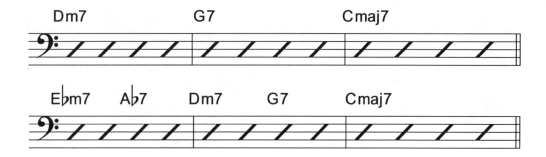

The standard "Take the A Train" provides an opportunity to reharmonize by replacing Dm7-G7 (measures 5 and 6) with a quick II-V sequence (Ebm7-Ab7, Dm7-G7).

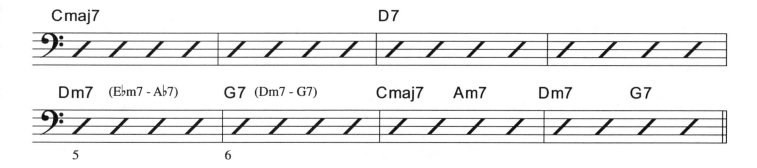

Alternative Starting Notes

As you become more familiar with the patterns in this book you will want to start experimenting, Here are a few fun and challenging exercises using blues changes. Instead of playing 1 on the first beat, try the 9, ♭7, 5 or 3 as indicated by the numbers above the measures. If there is not a number, start the measure with the root (1). When substituting these intervals, work your way back to 1 within the next few beats as in measures 3 and 4 of exercise #1. This will help the listeners and remind the soloists where they are in the form of the song.

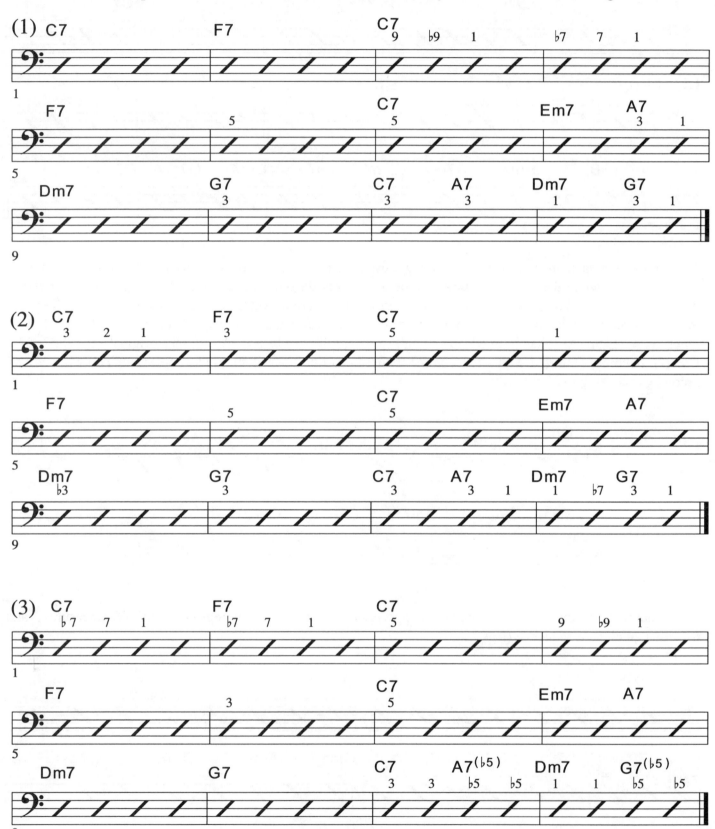

42

Here you will find one of several ways to play the exercises on the previous page. Cover this page as you work on page 42. Use it to check your ideas. Remember you are training your ear. You will prefer some patterns over others. I've found it wise to stick to the root on beat one for the first few choruses. The examples below give you more options as you get further into the song. Try not to get too "outside." The soloist may be listening to you for the form of the song.

Added Notes

When improvising walking lines, repeated quarter notes can become boring no matter how creative you might be harmonically. Putting in fills or added rhythmic figures will make your lines interesting and help to create a groove. You can do this by adding eighth notes and triplet figures. In swing, eighth notes are interpreted as a triplet figure. For example, Figure 1 would be played as Figure 2. You are stretching the first note and following it with a shorter second note. Of course, the faster the tempo, the harder it is to create this "long-short" feel. Figure 3 shows another technique bass players use called the "dead note." It is a percussive technique where the second note does not sound as a specific pitch. You simply lay all four fingers of your left hand lightly over the strings while the right hand picks the string. The notes used for the full triplet fill, as in Figure 4, are often taken from the chord. Arpeggiate the chord you are walking over and you will have many possibilities for triplet runs. Try placing two back to back. There are no rules as to where they should be placed. Have fun and try not to be predictable.

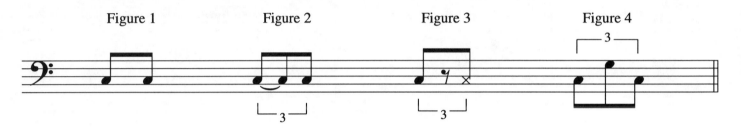

Straight quarter note walking pattern

Using "dead notes"

Eighth note fills should be played with a triplet feel

Triplet fills with added notes taken from the C triad

Blues (Ray Brown)

Ray Brown is a master of the walking bass. His use of added notes keeps the lines interesting and fresh. Notice the placement of his fills. They can be found on every beat. Remember to interpret the eighth note figure as a triplet. In many cases the second note is implied and not solidly struck. Also, notice his unique harmonic concept. He wisely uses half steps and whole steps in his approach to a new chord.

45

Part Two

Part Two contains twenty familiar standards. You have already studied the first seven. These songs were chosen because they are called frequently, and contain most of the problems you will encounter. Use the first half of the book as a reference. Take the time to look up any questions you might have. You will find page numbers under selected measures. You will learn faster and become a more accomplished player if you spend time learning the patterns. As you have seen, some exercises require more effort than others. This is also the case with many songs. Some chord progressions are more complex. Connecting chords with a cleverly designed walking line is an art.

A Few Things To Remember:

- Make all large jumps between beats 1 and 2 or 3 and 4.
- When descending from major 7th chord, make the 7th natural.
- If you see a chord with nothing specific behind it, treat it as a Major 7 chord.
- Treat a Six chord as a Major 7 chord. ex. C6 = Cmaj7 when walking.
- When walking over more than one measure using the same chord, aim for the 5th or a strong note harmonically for the first beat of the new measure.
- When descending, the ♭6 makes an excellent passing tone.
- Memorize the chord progression. Referring to chords by their corresponding number (in relation to the key) will help you to remember the changes.
- Memorize the melody. For copyright reasons, melodies have not been included in this book. Find the music and learn the melody. Knowing the melody helps greatly if you are trying to memorize the chords. It is also a great aid if you are just learning how to solo. Many great jazz artists started out by planning their solo ideas around the melody.
- Learn the modes. Not all, but many of the patterns found in this book are based on the modes.
- Always know where you are in the form of the song. ex. AABA
- Rhythmically placing emphasis on beats 2 and 4 (back beats) will help you create a steadier groove.
- Have fun with added notes, but don't overuse them.
- Find a teacher who has a background in jazz. Most music stores around the country have a good rock bass teacher, but not all have experience in playing jazz.
- Listen to many different jazz bassists. Play along with recordings.
- Find some players who are eager to learn. Get together and read charts. Use your ears as well as your brain. The patterns found in this book will get you started. It is designed to train your ear. When you are comfortable, experiment.

Have a daily practice routine. Divide your practice time into two parts. First; warm up. Use the diatonic (based on the natural scale) exercises found at the end of the book. Start slowly and increase the tempo as you get stronger. As you become familiar with the diatonic exercises and modes, make up your own patterns. Write them down. Remember, the scale patterns shown and the patterns you make up should be practiced in all twelve keys. Second; learn the walking patterns. If you are a slow reader, use the intervals (numbers). Play each pattern several times. Look away from the music and play it several more times. By committing the patterns to memory and using the numbers (intervals), transposing the patterns will be a breeze. When practicing with the recording, listen to how everything fits together, the patterns and the chord structure. Make thinking in terms of intervals a habit. It will save you hours on the gig, at rehearsal or in the studio if someone decides to change the key of the song you are preforming. You wont have to write out a new chart.

Part Three gives you written example lines for the standards. Use them as reading exercises. Test yourself by writing the intervals above the notes. Remember the intervals should correspond to the chord above. ex. Cmaj7, C - 1, D - 2, E - 3, etc.

Standard #1

(Similar to "Take the A Train")

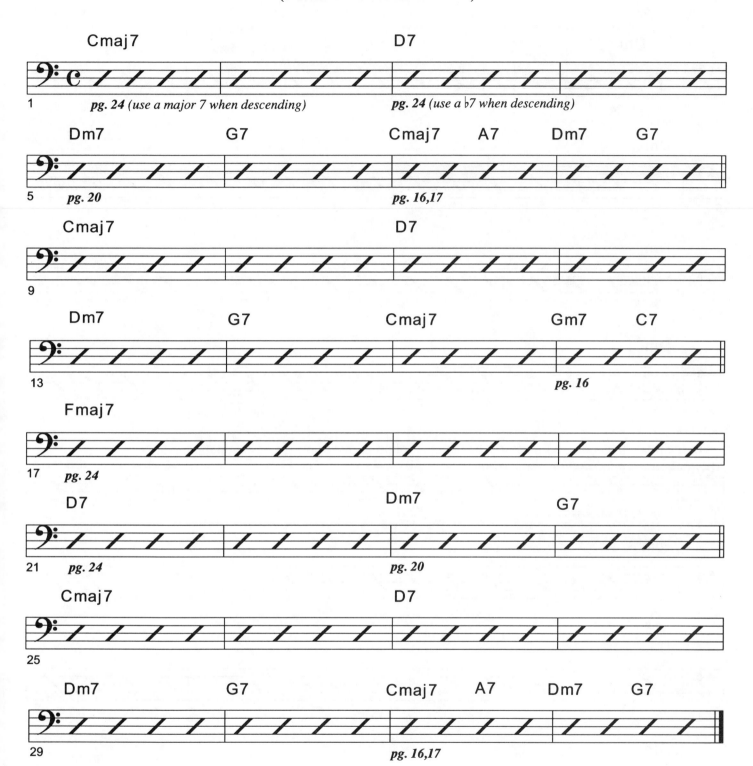

Standard #2

(Similar to "So What")

Dm

| | | | |

1   *pg. 26*

Dm

| | | | |

5

Dm

| | | | |

9

Dm

| | | | |

13

E♭m

| | | | |

17   *pg. 26 (transpose up 1/2 step)*

E♭m

| | | | |

21

Dm

| | | | |

25

Dm

| | | | |

29

Standard #3

(Similar to "Autumn Leaves")

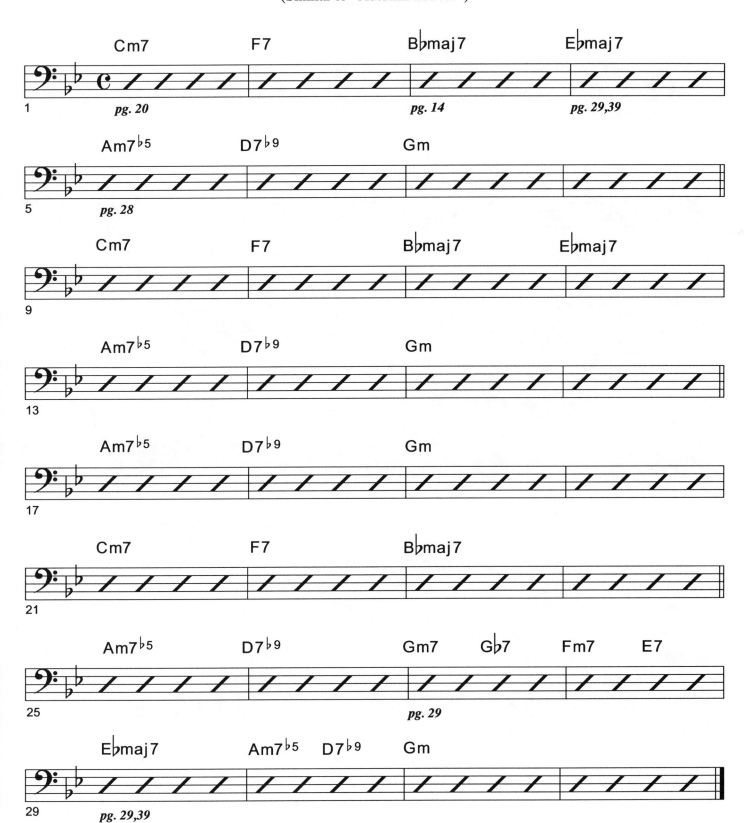

Standard #4 (3/4 Blues)

(Similar to "All Blues")

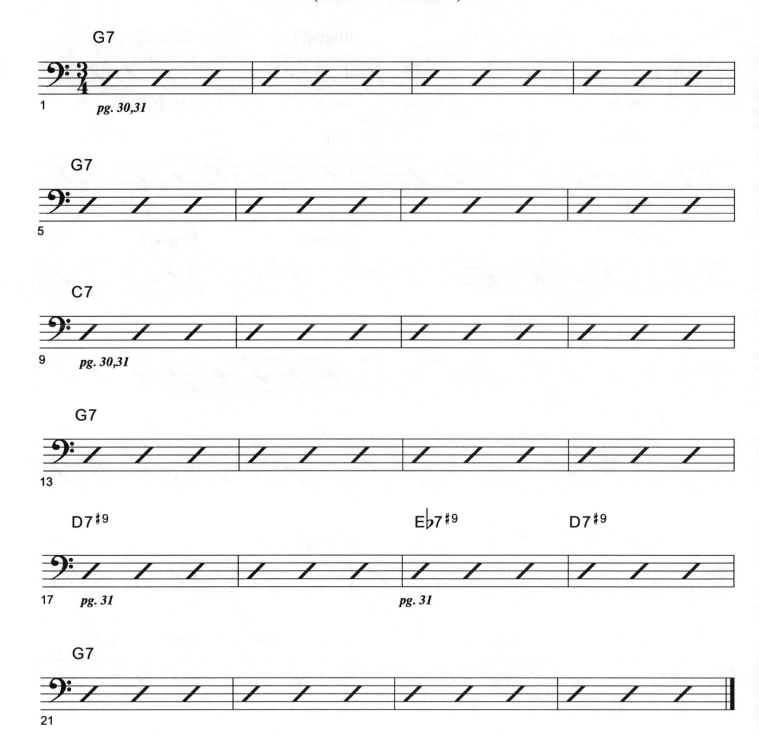

Standard #5 - A Jazz Waltz

(Similar to "Someday My Prince Will Come")

Standard #6

(Similar to "Just The Way You Look Tonight")

Standard #7

(Similar to "Night and Day")

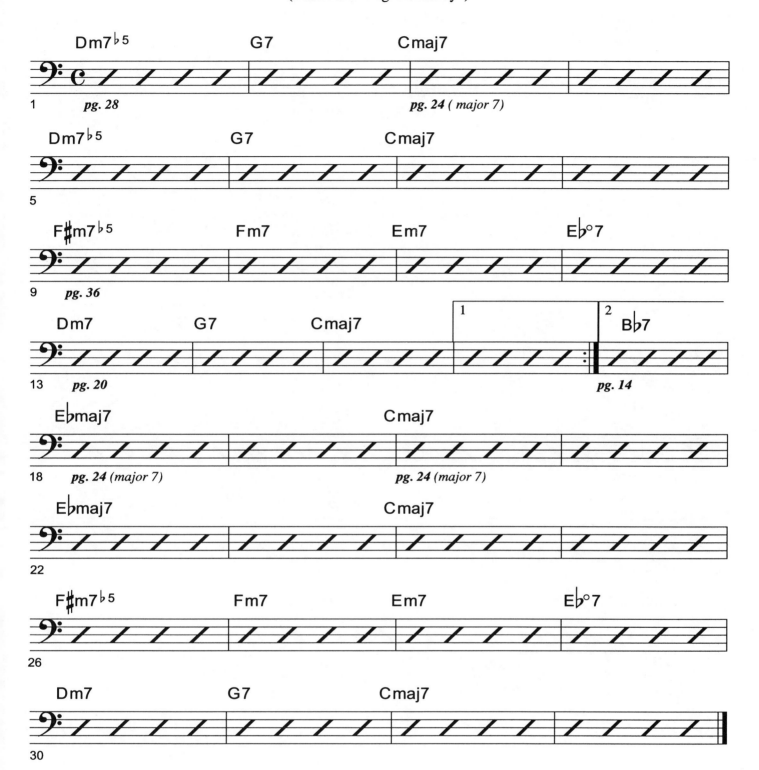

Standard #8

(Similar to "All Of Me")

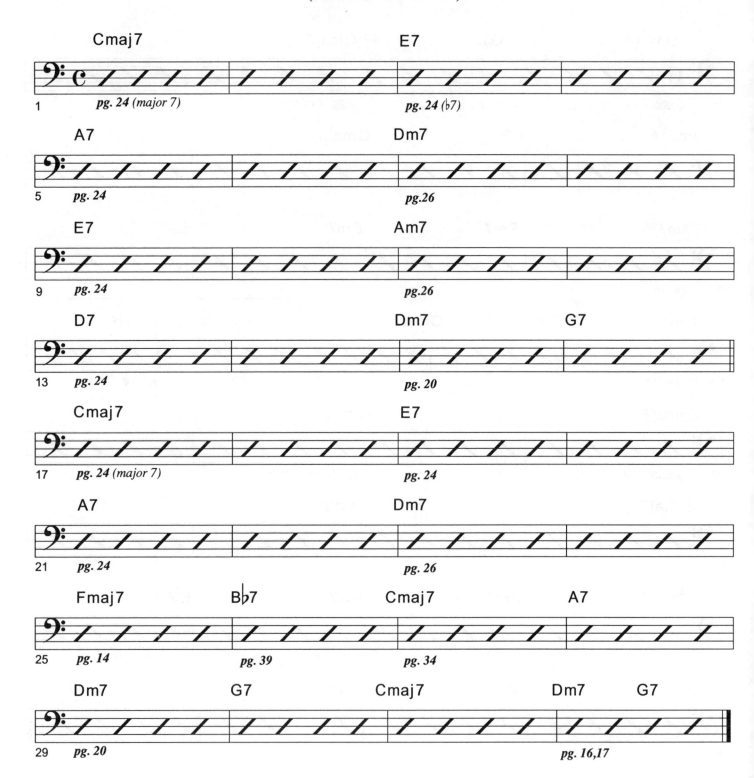

Standard #9

(Similar to "Satin Doll")

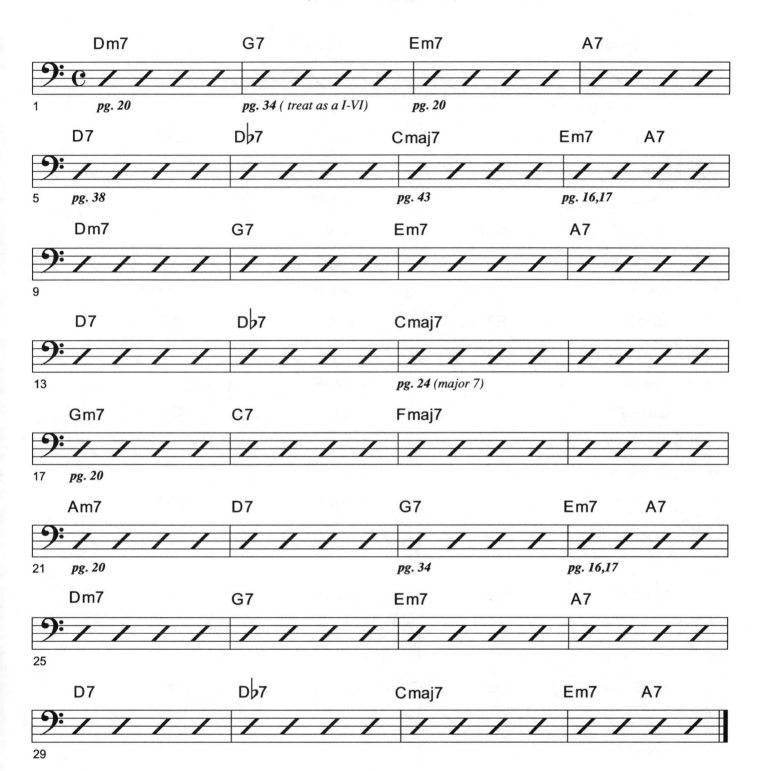

Standard #10

(Similar to "How High The Moon" and "Ornithology")

Standard #11

(Similar to "Out Of Nowhere")

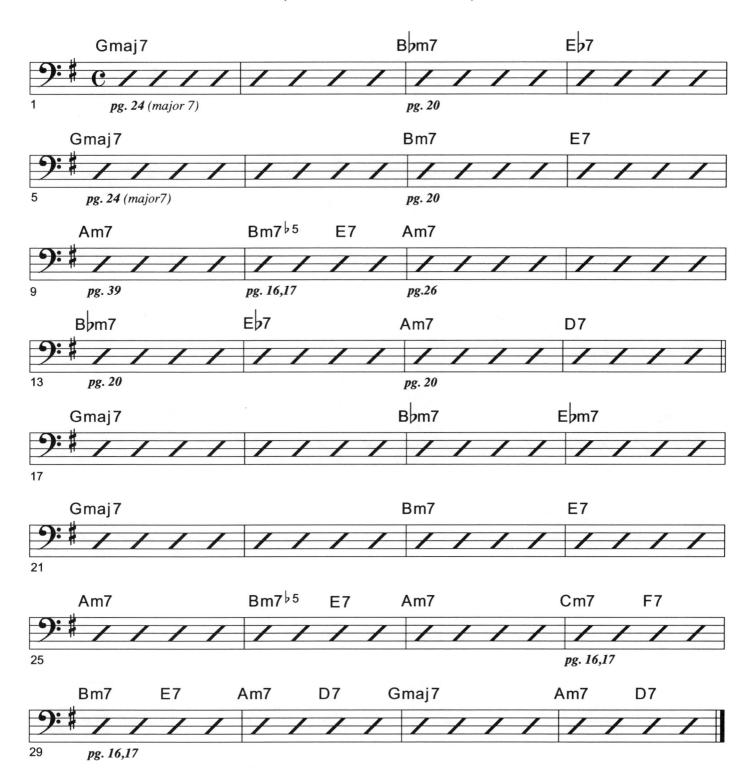

Standard #12

(Similar to "Days Of Wine And Roses")

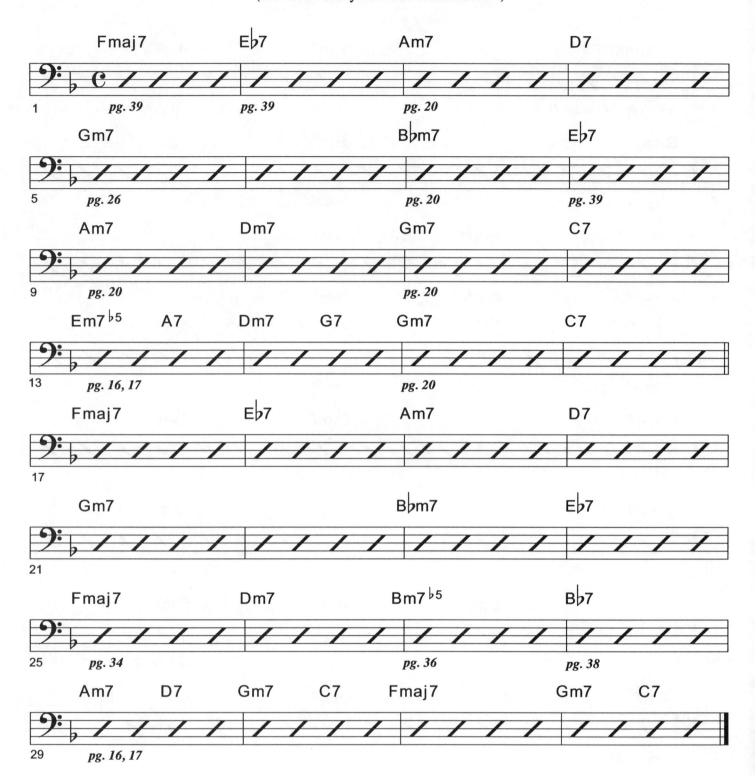

Standard #13

(Similar to "All The Things You Are")

Standard #14

(Similar to "Donna Lee" and "Indiana")

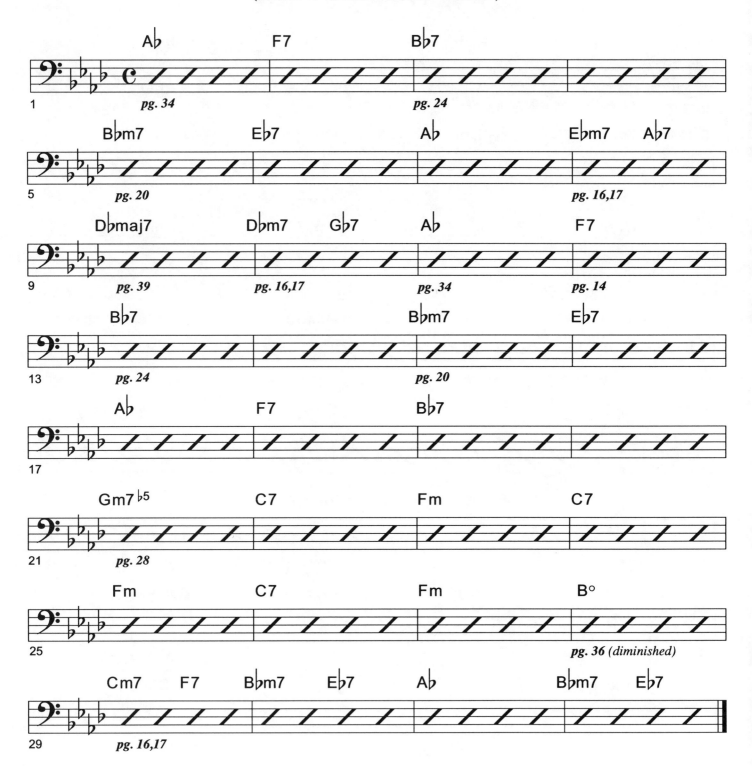

Standard #15

(Similar to "There'll Never Be Another You")

Standard #16

(Similar to "What Is This Thing Called Love")

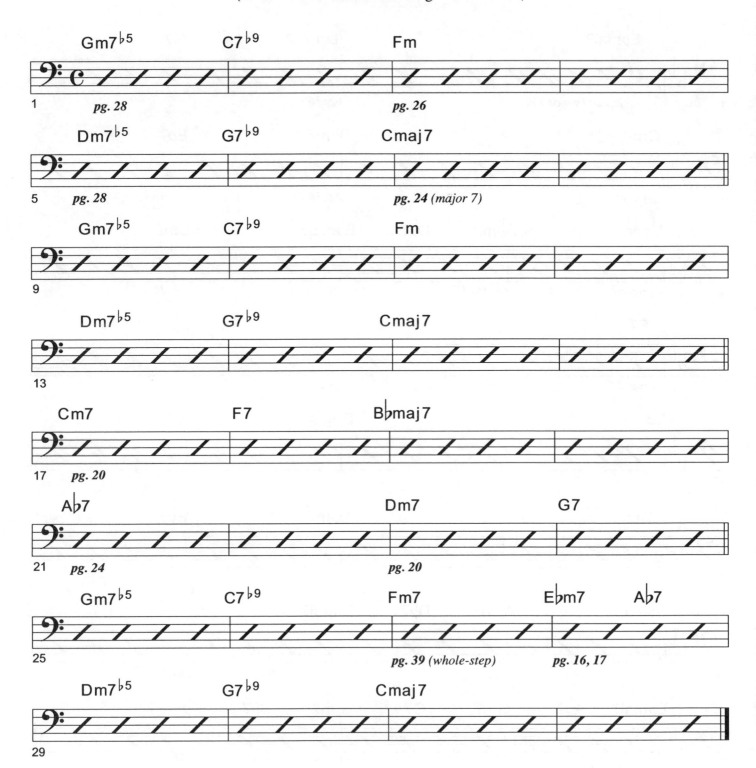

Standard #17

(Similar to "Stella")

Standard #18

(Similar to "A Night In Tusinia")

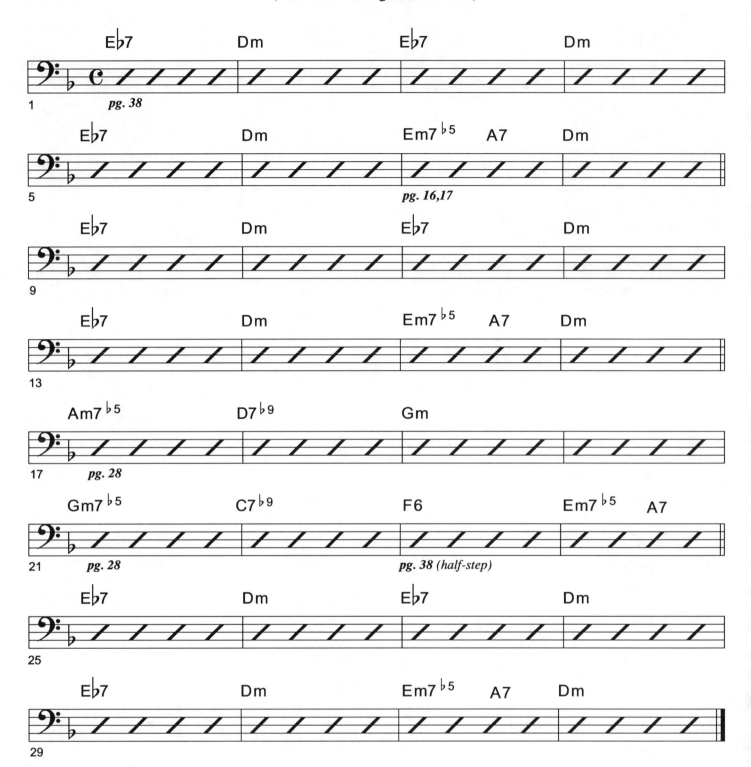

Standard #19

(Similar to "Cherokee")

Standard #20

(Similar to "Giant Steps")

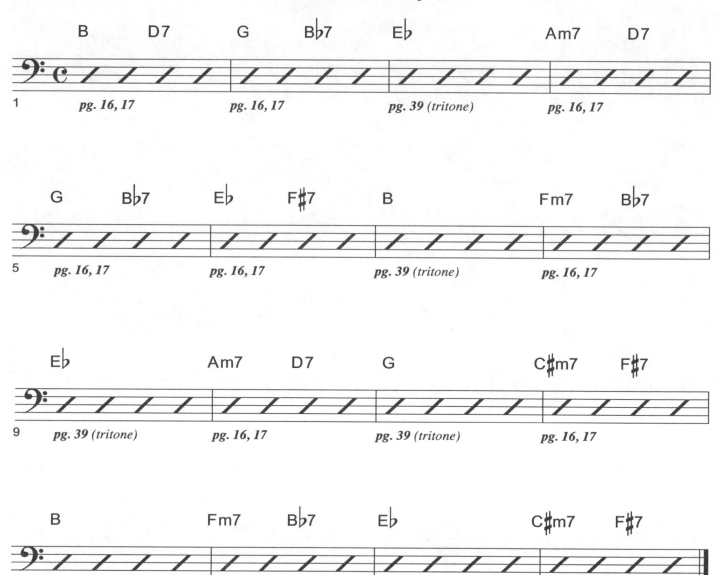

Part Three

The following section contains written versions of the 20 standards found in the book. Many of the patterns you have practiced have been included. Use this section to check your ideas or to get new ideas. Go back to **Part Two** and try them out. Review the patterns found in **Part One**. Listen to the recording. The chord progressions will become more familiar to you as you practice them. Your ear will tell you what works and what does not work. Memorize the chord changes.

Start training your ear. Listen to as many bass players as you can (pg. 96). Pick out players you like and study their ideas. If you like their tone, try to match the sound. Transcribe walking lines from recordings. Like anything else, the more transcriptions you do, the faster you will become at hearing the lines. Start with Oscar Pettiford or Ray Brown. Their lines are easy to hear and show a contrasting style. Have a goal. Transcribe a little every day as part of your practice routine. Your practice habits will dictate your rate of progress.

Standard #1

(Similar to "Take the A Train")

Standard #2

(Similar to "So What")

Standard #3

(Similar to "Autumn Leaves")

Standard #4 (3/4 Blues)

(Similar to "All Blues")

Standard #5 - A Jazz Waltz

(Similar to "Someday My Prince Will Come")

Standard #6

(Similar to "Just The Way You Look Tonight")

Standard #7

(Similar to "Night and Day")

Standard #8

(Similar to "All of Me")

Standard #9

(Similar to "Satin Doll")

Standard #10

(Similar to "How High The Moon" and "Ornithology")

Standard #11

(Similar to "Out of Nowhere")

Standard #12

(Similar to "Days of Wine and Roses")

Standard #13

(Similar to "All The Things You Are")

Standard #14

(Similar to "Donna Lee" and "Indiana")

Standard #15

(Similar to "There'll Never Be Another You")

Standard #16

(Similar to "What Is This Thing Called Love")

Standard #17

(Similar to "Stella")

Standard #18

(Similar to "A Night In Tunisia")

Standard #19

(Similar to "Cherokee")

Standard #20

(Similar to "Giant Steps")

Blues - Variations

Basic Three-Chord Blues

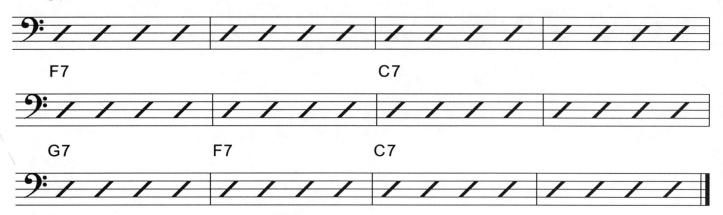

Adding the IV chord in bar 2 and the V chord in bar 12

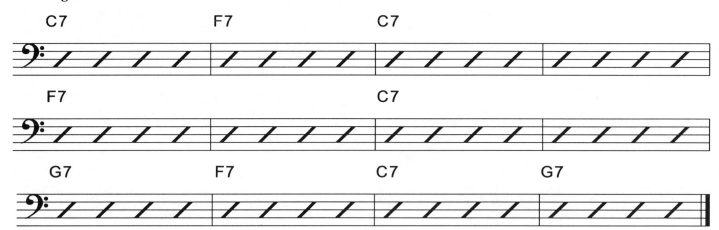

Adding II -Vs

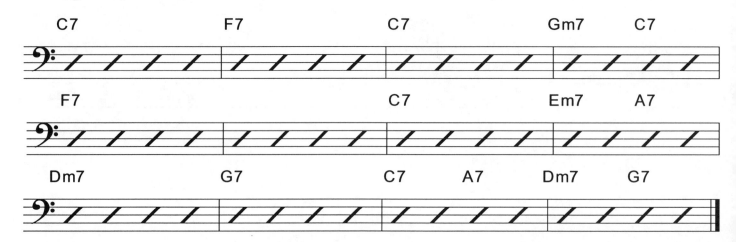

Parker Blues Starting on the Major I chord and descending with a series of II -Vs

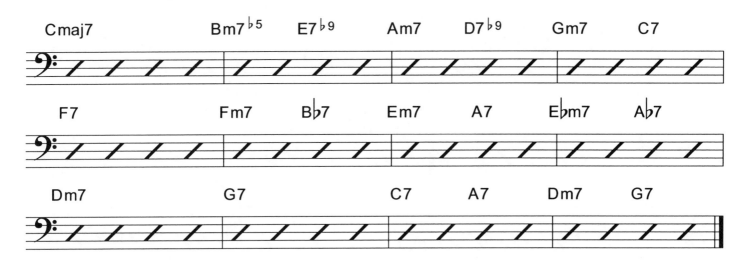

Another variation starting on C# and going around the cycle of fifths, leading to the F7 chord in the fifth bar.

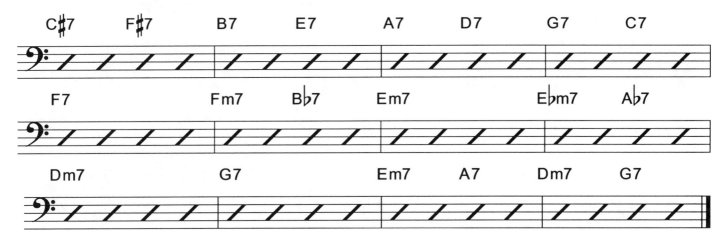

Minor Blues

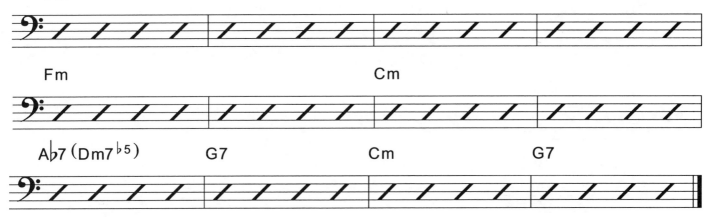

Rhythm Changes - Variations

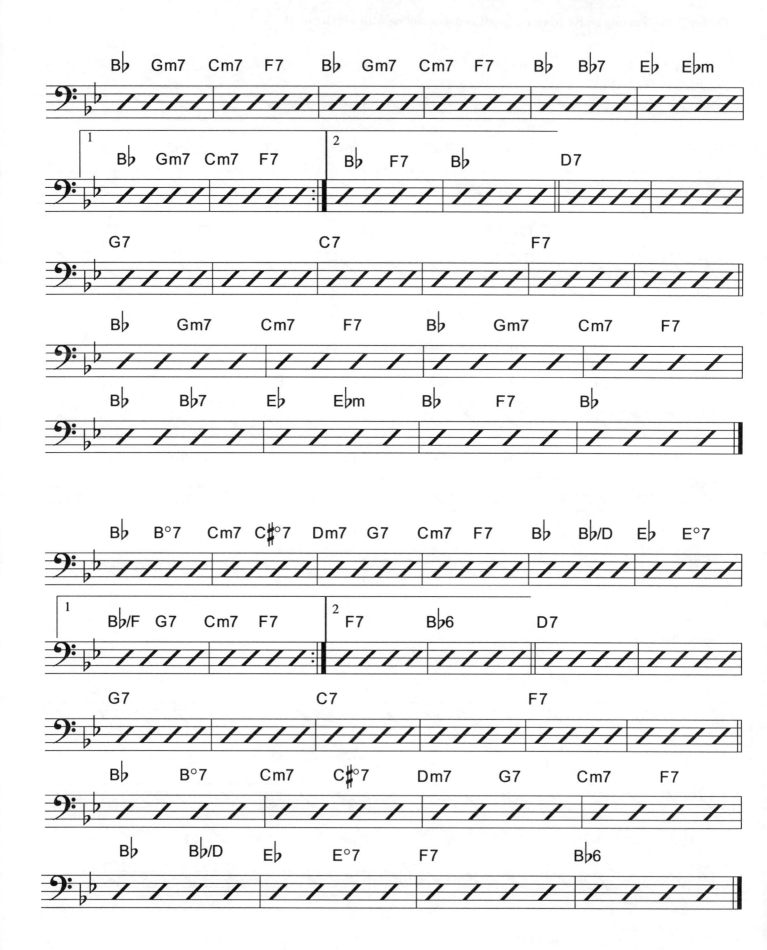

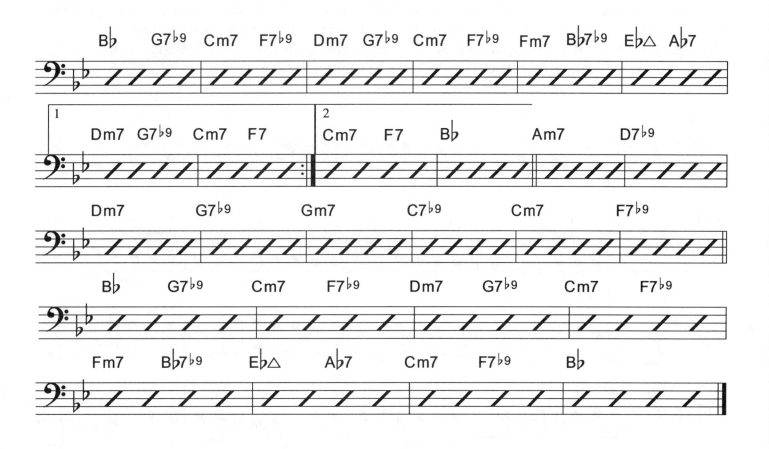

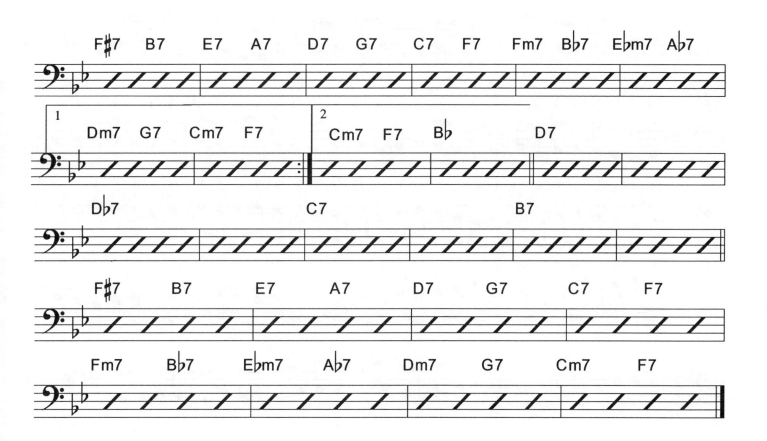

A Daily Exercise

Here are two exercises based on the G major scale. G major works well because you can use closed position (no open strings) on the electric bass. Follow the suggested fingering. After memorizing each exercise, play them in the keys of A♭, A, B♭, B, C, etc. Spend at least 20 minutes warming up. On page 93 you will find more ideas based on the major scale. Memorize them and take each one through all twelve keys.

Scale Form Patterns

(1) **G Major**

(2) **Diatonic 3rds**

(3) **Diatonic Triplets**

(4) **Diatonic 7th Chord**

(5) **Triplet Exercise**

(6) **Triplet Variation**

(7) **7th Chord Variation**

(8) **Diatonic 4ths**

Modes of the Major Scale

On this page you will find seven different versions of the C major scale. Modes are comprised of scales taken from the pitches of other scales. Each scale is unique and used for improvising solos and developing walking lines. The modes shown here start on a different interval based on the C major scale. Practice these modes and learn to identify them by their sound quality. Remembering the modes can be made simple by playing the white keys on the piano and visualizing them. Make up your own practice exercises using the modes. Write them down. Learn them in all twelve keys.

Ionian

Intervals - 1 2 3 4 5 6 7 1

Dorian

1 2 ♭3 4 5 6 ♭7 1

Phrygian

1 ♭2 ♭3 4 5 ♭6 ♭7 1

Lydian

1 2 3 ♯4 5 6 7 1

Mixolydian

1 2 3 4 5 6 ♭7 1

Aeolian

1 2 ♭3 4 5 ♭6 ♭7 1

Locrian

1 ♭2 ♭3 4 ♭5 ♭6 ♭7 1

Recommended Song List

This list includes the songs most frequently called today. Use it as a beginning list. Some band leaders do not mind players reading from a book. Others prefer you to have the songs memorized. Memorizing changes is easier if you remember the chords as numbers (intervals), know the melody and be in a situation where you can perform the songs. If you are just starting out, play with recordings. Anything and everything will help. Compare this list to others, start your own list and keep adding to the songs you know. (* indicates standards found in the book with similar chord structure)

Jazz Standards

A Foggy Day
All Of Me *
All The Things You Are *
Alone Together
A Night In Tunisia *
Autumn Leaves *
Autunm in New York
Blue Skies
Broadway
But Not For Me
Bye Bye Blackbird
Caravan
Cherokee *
C-Jam Blues
Days Of Wine And Roses *
Donna Lee *
Don't Get Around Much
East Of The Sun
End Of A Love Affair
Falling In Love With Love
Four
Fly Me To The Moon
Getting Sentimental Over You
Giant Steps *
Gone With The Wind
Green Dolphin Street
Groovin' High
Have You Met Miss Jones
Honeysuckle Rose
How High The Moon *
I Get A Kick Out Of You
I Got Rhythm
I'll Remember April
I Remember You
I Love You
In A Mellow Tone
Indiana *
In The Mood
Invitation
It Had To Be You
It Could Happen To You
It Don't Mean A Thing
It's Alright With Me
Joy Spring
Just Friends
Just In Time
Just One Of Those Things
Lady Be Good
Lady Is A Tramp
Like Someone In Love
L.O.V.E.

Love For Sale
Love Walked In
Lullaby Of Birdland
Makin' Woopie
Moonglow
My Romance
My Secret Love
My Shining Hour
Night And Day *
No Greater Love
Oleo (Rhythm Changes)
Ornithology *
Our Love Is Here To Stay
Out Of Nowhere *
Paper Moon
Pennies From Heaven
Perdido
Preacher, The
Route 66
St. Louis Blues
Satin Doll *
Scrapple From The Apple
Secret Love
Sentimental Journey
September In The Rain
Softly As In A Morning Sunrise
So What *
Speak Low
Star Eyes
Stella By Starlight *
Stolen Moments
Stompin At Savoy
Stormy Weather
Straight, No Chaser
Sunny Side Of The Street
Sweet Georgia Brown
S' Wonderful
Take Five
Take The A Train *
Tangerine
Takin' A Chance On Love
There'll Never Be Another You *
The Way You Look Tonight *
Undecided
What Is This Thing Called Love *
Where Or When
World On A String
Yardbird Suite
Yesterdays
You Stepped Out Of A Dream
You Took Advantage Of Me

Ballads

As Time Goes By
A Time For Love
Bewitched
Body & Soul
But Beautiful
Come Rain Or Come Shine
Darn That Dream
Don't Blame Me
Dream
Embraceable You
Everything Happens To Me
Ghost Of A Chance
Here's That Rainy Day
How Deep Is The Ocean
I Can't Get Started
I Got It Bad
In a Sentimental Mood
I Thought About You
Laura
Lover Man
Lush Life
Misty
Mood Indigo
Moonlight In Vermont
More I See You, The
My Foolish Heart
My Funny Valentine
Nearness Of You
Once In A While
Over The Rainbow
Polka Dots and Moonbeams
Prelude To A Kiss
Round Midnight
Since I Fell For You
Skylark
Smoke Gets In Your Eyes
Someone To Watch Over Me
Sophisticated Lady
Summertime
Teach Me Tonight
Tenderly
That's All
Two For The Road
Very Thought Of You
What's New
When I Fall In Love
When Sunny Gets Blue
Yesterdays

Latin

Black Orpheus
Blue Bossa
Ceora
Desafinado
Gentle Rain
Girl From Impanema
How Insensitive
Meditation
Once I Loved
One Note Samba
Quiet Nights
Shadow Of Your Smile
So Many Stars
Song For My Father
Spain
St. Thomas
Triste
Watch What Happens
Wave

3/4 (Waltz)

A Child Is Born
Always
All Blues *
Blusette
Emily
Gravy Waltz
Moon River
Footprints
My Favorite Things
Tenderly
Someday My Prince Will Come *
Up Jumped Spring

Bass Players

New Orleans
Pops Foster, John Lindsay, Steve Brown, Bill Johnson

Early Swing
Milt Hinton, Bob Haggart, Walter Page, John Kirby, Israel Crosby, Artie Bernstein, John Simmons

Ellington's Bassists
Wellman Braud, Billy Taylor, Hayes Alvis, Jimmie Blanton, Junior Raglin, Oscar Pettiford

Swing To Bebop
Oscar Pettiford, Ray Brown, Slam Stewart, George Duvivier, Red Callender, Curley Russell, Nelson Boyd, Tommy Potter

Hard Bop To Cool
Paul Chambers, Charles Mingus, Wilbur Ware, Percy Heath, Red Mitchell, Monty Budwig, Leroy Vinnegar

Post Bop To Free Jazz
Scott LaFaro, Sam Jones, Richard Davis, Art Davis, Jimmy Garrison, Reggie Workman, Israel Crosby, Gary Peacock, Charlie Haden, Davis Izenson

Modal Jazz
Ron Carter, Dave Holland

Contemtorary Bassists
Eddie Gomez, Neils-Henning Orsted Pedersen, Stanley Clark, George Mraz, Michael Moore, Ray Drummond, John Heard, Reggie Johnson, Bob Magnusson, Rufus Reed, Joco Pastorius, John Clayton, Brian Bromberg, Avishai Cohen, Jay Leonhart, Christian McBride, John Patitucci, Todd Coolman, Victor Wooten

Jay Hungerford

Jay Hungerford is a graduate of Southern Illinois University at Carbondale with a degree in Music Education. He has taught at the University of Missouri in St. Louis, Meramec College, Fontbonne College and has been a member of the Jazz faculty at Webster University in St. Louis for over 20 years. He currently travels the jazz festival circuit with several west coast bands. Other performance credits include Herb Ellis, Buddy Defranco, Eddie Higgins, Roger Williams, Maynard Ferguson, Scott Hamilton, Bill Watrous, Carl Fontana, Warren Vache', Mike Vax and Bobby Shew. Jay performs with the St. Louis Symphony "Pops" concerts, and the Muny Orchestra during the summer. He can be heard on numerous contemporary Christian recordings. His most recent CD, *The Keys to the City*, includes 14 of the top jazz pianists in St. Louis in a duo format. Jay also plays bass full time at Grace Church in Maryland Heights, Missouri. Jay plays a '64 Fender Jazz Bass, a Yamaha BB5000A 5-string, a Yamaha Silent bass and an early John Juzek upright bass.